Princess Prunella
AND THE Purple Peanut

MARGARET ATWOOD
Illustrated by MARYANN KOVALSKI

KPk
Key Porter Kids

Canadian Cataloguing in Publication Data

Atwood, Margaret, 1939-
Princess Prunella and the Purple Peanut
ISBN 1-55013-732-8
I. Kovalski, Maryann. II. Title.

PS8501.T86P7 1995   jC813'.54   C95-931577-2

PZ7.A78Pr 1995

A portion of the author's proceeds will be donated to The Woodcock Fund.

The publisher gratefully acknowledges the assistance of the Canada Council, the Ontario Publishing Centre and the Government of Ontario.

Key Porter kids
is an imprint of
Key Porter Books Limited
70 The Esplanade
Toronto, Ontario
Canada M5E 1R2

Printed and bound in China

95 96 97 98 99 5 4 3 2 1

For my mother, who read to me
And my daughter, who got read to

M.A.

To Gregory, Jenny and Joanna

M.K.

rincess Prunella lived in a pink palace with her pinheaded
parents, Princess Patty and Prince Peter, her three plump pussycats,
Patience, Prue and Pringle, and her puppydog, Pug.

Princess Prunella was proud, prissy and pretty, and unhappily very spoiled. She would never pick up her playthings, plump her pillows, or put away her pens, pencils and puzzles. Instead, after her breakfast of prunes and porridge, and her pineapple and passion-fruit punch, presented in a copper cup painted with porpoises and spiders, she would parade around all day, in puffy petticoats sprinkled with sparkling pink sequins, a peculiar pilly polo-necked pullover, a pair of pale purple pumps with peonies on the insteps, and a pinafore printed with pansies and petunias, slurping peppermints and peering at her dimples in a pocket mirror. "I am perfectly pretty," she would say. "When I grow up I will marry a pinheaded prince with piles of pin-money, who will praise me and pamper me, and adore me as much as I do."

Princess Prunella had a problem perceiving where she was going, because of the pocket mirror. At supper it was hard for her to place the spoon precisely between her lips, so she spilled parsley and potatoes on her pinafore, producing spots.

She upset the pudgy palace lamps from their pedestals patterned with puffins and pelicans, bumped into the parlour piano draped with pewter-coloured polyester periwinkles, tripped over the powdered porcelain Pekingese perched near the fireplace, and tipped Princess Patty's powerful perfume all over the Persian carpet, making an unpleasant puddle.

"Princess Prunella! Pray pay attention!" said the palace parlourmaid, Penny. "And please do not leave peppermint wrappers in the potted palms."

"Pooh, Penny," replied Prunella peevishly. "Who gives a piffle what you think? You are nothing but a paid servant. Plod off and get the scrub pail, and wipe up that puddle of poisonous perfume."

She stepped on the tails of the plump pussycats, Patience, Prue and Pringle.

"Pardon ME," said Patience.

"You are not polite," said Prue.

"Psst," said Pringle.

"Oh, don't pester, you parasitical pipsqueaks," said Princess Prunella. "Pussycats are perverse, piddling, pointy-pawed, pie-faced pudding-brains. They are not worth spit."

She stomped on the paw of her puppydog, Pug.
"Pain! Pain!" howled Pug, his pupils protruding.
"Stupid puppy," snapped Prunella. "What a performance!
Don't pretend to be in pain. And next time, get out of my path."

One April day, a white-haired wrinkly-wristed Wise Woman, in a sparse but pristine pleated petticoat, paper slippers and an imperfectly patched wrap, tapped at the door. Princess Prunella opened it because she was going out anyway, with her purse full of peppermints and spinning a parasol, so she could prance around in the pale spring sunlight and get a better view of her perfect dimples in her pocket mirror. "What do you want?" she snapped.

"Please, Princess," said the Wise Woman. "I am just a poor person. Could I have a piece of leftover porridge, or a peppermint, or a used prune if you could spare one?"

"You are interrupting me," said Prunella. "Porridge and prunes and peppermints are for princesses. Poor people don't deserve any. So get away from this palace, you pathetic peasant pauper."

The Wise Woman was not pleased. "Appearances are deceptive," she said. "You are not pretty inside, just as I am not poor. I had heard you were spoiled and stuck-up, but I preferred to see for myself. Now I am going to put a spell on you. It will never disappear until you perform three Good Deeds."

Then she waggled her white wrinkly wrists and pronounced impressively. "Nipity Pipity Zeenut,

Let the princess sprout a peanut."

"Pooh pooh," said Prunella, tossing her long, perfectly permed hair, which had a pink primrose pinned in it. "I don't care a paltry particle." And she pushed the white-haired wrinkly-wristed Wise Woman off the palace porch and pulled the door shut.

But the next time she peeked into her pocket mirror, there was
a purple peanut the size of a pea, right on the tip of her nose.
"How putrid!" she said. "I am no longer perfect!" And she began to weep.

"Never mind, Prunella my pet," said her pinheaded but practical parent Princess Patty. "Purple peanuts are temporary. It will pop, and disappear."

And for supper she fed Prunella some parsley and paprika soup, a pile of potted pigeon and pike and pickerel pancakes, and some pepper and porridge preserve, on a pretty plate patterned with pendulous poppies.

But the next day the purple peanut was still there. Now it was as big as a peach pit. Prunella put a plaster of puffballs and parsnips on it, but this did not work. She ordered up a pepperoni and marzipan pizza and some popcorn and pickles, with a piece of pecan and pickerel pie for dessert, to help her feel better, but this did not work either.

"How impossible! This is worse than chicken pox or mumps! Now I will never marry a pinheaded prince with piles of pin-money," she pouted. "What prince, however pinheaded, would want a princess with a purple peanut as big as a peach pit on her nose?"

The three pussycats purred. "Serves you right for being a selfish pig," they said. Prunella wept herself to sleep, with a pillow over her head.

In the morning the three plump pussycats poked and pinched Princess Prunella awake with their pointy paws. "We pity you," they whispered. "Your eyes are all pink and puffy, and that purple peanut is as big as a pumpkin. So we will remind you of what the white-haired wrinkly-wristed Wise Woman said: Perform three Good Deeds and your purple peanut will pop."

"What are Good Deeds?" said Prunella.

"You are a perverse pie-faced pudding-brain," said the three pussycats politely, padding pompously away on their polished paws. "You should have paid more attention!"

Princess Prunella paced pensively across the Persian carpet, attempting to
think up Good Deeds. She could not think of any, so she went out onto the patio
with her parasol and her purse full of peppermints.

"I have been a proud, presumptuous and preoccupied princess," she
pronounced; and a pearly teardrop plopped sloppily onto her spotted pocket hanky.

Then she perceived five parti-coloured parrots pouncing on the petticoats, pinafores and puce-coloured pantaloons that Penny, the palace parlourmaid, had pinned with pegs to the parapet. "If I don't prevent those pouncing parrots from pecking perforations in the petticoats, pinafores and pantaloons, Penny will be up to her armpits in trouble," thought Prunella. So she prodded the parrots away with her parasol.

The purple peanut grew smaller. But Princess Prunella did not notice, because she saw her prize puppydog, Pug, being pursued by a poisonous puff-pig. There was a large population of these, perennially prowling around among the porcupines, partridges and painted turtles in the nearby plantation of poplars and passionflowers.

"Pug! Pug! Do not despair!" she cried, and pelted after the puff-pig as fast as she could go, picking up pebbles and propelling them at it with all her power. The petrified puff-pig plopped down, and Prunella scooped up Pug, whose pulse was pounding and who was panting with panic, patted him, and fed him a peppermint. The purple peanut grew smaller, but Princess Prunella did not notice, because for once she was thinking about someone other than herself.

Princess Prunella proceeded down the path, towards the palace pond. There, while stepping around an apple sapling, she saw a pear-shaped, pinheaded prince about to plunge in among the plastic lily-pads, sporting a plaid pyjama top and a pair of preposterous plum-coloured polka-dotted pants.

"Prince! Prince!" she called. "Don't plunge! That pond is polluted! Also it is full of ponderous pointy-toothed pike, which will probably eat you!"

"You have preserved my life, Princess," said the pear-shaped, pinheaded prince. "Your prudent personality is a praiseworthy and precious pearl. As princes go I am practically a pauper, with almost no pin-money, but when you are older perhaps I might be prepared to propose."

"But surely that is not possible," said Prunella unhappily.

"Why not?" said the pinheaded prince placidly, with his hands in his preposterous plum-coloured polka-dotted pants pockets.

"Because of the purple peanut as big as a pumpkin on the tip of my nose," said Prunella, who had just remembered it. She was not predisposed to accept this particular prince as her life partner, although he was properly apparelled and partially presentable; she no longer cared about pin-money; but she pined for a particle of her previous self-respect.

"There is no purple peanut," said the prince, peering.

And it was true. The purple peanut had disappeared.

The plump pussycats, perched in the pear tree, purred with rapture, Penny the palace parlormaid applauded, and the white-haired wrinkly-wristed Wise Woman, who had been peeping from behind a potted palm on the patio, pronounced her approval of Princess Prunella's three positive performances.

Even the pinheaded
parents, Princess Patty and Prince
Peter, who had spoiled Prunella in
the first place, were pleased.

"It is an improvement to be with a person who is not peering into a pocket
mirror all the time, especially at supper, when we are having pheasant pie with
whipped turnip surprise, and papaya pasta, and parsnip pinwheels, and parchment and
pumpernickel pastries," they said. "It is more polite."

And for once, although pinheaded, they were right.